William B. Eerdmans Publishing Company
Grand Rapids, Michigan

CHAYNA

© Copyright 1986 by Scandinavia
Publishing House, Nørregade 32, DK-1165 Copenhagen K.
English language edition first published 1987
through special arrangement with Scandinavia
by W. B. Eerdmans Publishing Co.,
255 Jefferson Ave. S.E. Grand Rapids, Michigan 49503

Printed in Singapore

ISBN 0-8028-5021-9

CHAYNA
The Girl No One Wanted

Henri Nissen & F. Engsig-Karup

Chayna was chosen as the subject of this book from among thousands of children in Bangladesh by Filip Engsig-Karup, a **Santal** missionary, working in the area of Bangladesh where Chayna lives. Together, he and I wrote her story and took the photographs.

I first became acquainted with the work of Santal Mission in 1982 when I visited Bangladesh for the first time to write about DANIDA, the Danish government development project. Though I had grown up with a knowledge of mission efforts in the Third World, it was here in the small villages of Bangladesh that I became aware of the drastic social and spiritual renewal that the work of Christian missionaries can bring about. The purpose of this book will have been achieved by those of you who are not only touched by the story of Chayna, but who wish to become involved in the lives of children like her.

Henri Peter Nissen

William B. Eerdmans Publishing Company
Grand Rapids, Michigan

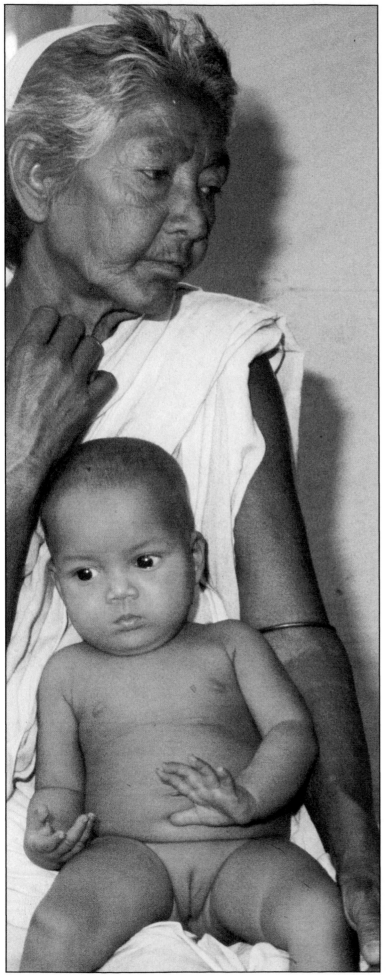

"**It's** a girl," sighed Grandmother when Oloka's and Trishna's little sister was born.

Father was waiting outside the straw hut. He shouted, "A girl? Oh no. Not another girl!"

"Yes, **Oke chayna! Chayna**!" answered Grandmother with a moan. "Chayna" means not wanted, not wanted at all, in **Bangla**, the language spoken in the part of Bangladesh where Chayna's family lives.

Mother was crying. Grandmother was crying. Oloka and Trishna were crying, too. The grownups were crying because the baby wasn't a boy. The children were crying, because the grownups cried, and because their father left the small wood hut and stormed off toward the village.

Two days later Father came home again. But he had been drinking too much rice wine. He was angry about the third baby girl in the family.

And that is why the new baby was called Chayna. She was the girl nobody wanted.

As the years went by, Chayna became sweet and smart. She began to understand why her father was unhappy with so many girls in the family.

In Bangladesh boys are thought to be more important than girls. There boys go to work with their fathers and learn a trade that will help them to earn money. Girls stay at home until they are married. A girl will usually marry when she is thirteen or fourteen years old. At that time her father will have to pay a lot of money to the man she marries.

Since Chayna's father had three daughters, he would have to pay a lot of money each time one of them married. And since he had no sons he would have no one to help him earn that money, and no one to support him when he grew old.

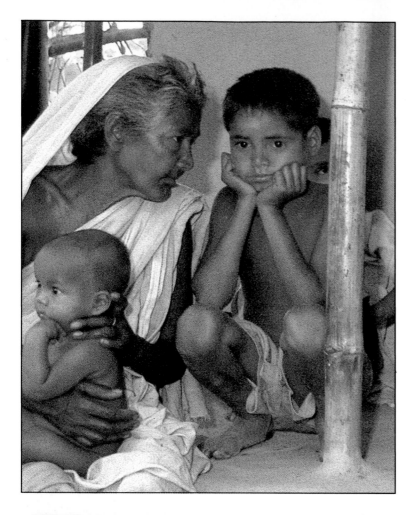

Chayna's mother hoped to have a baby boy someday. When, a few years after Chayna was born, her mother became pregnant again, everyone was excited. But the baby died the day it was born. Grandmother said, "It's good the baby died." The baby had been another little girl.

Oloka was glad Father did not leave home again that day and come back drunk. But he still didn't speak to anyone all day.

Chayna was feeling sorry for herself. "If only I had been a boy," she thought. "Then I could work, and Father would have been proud of me."

"It's just not fair," Chayna said out loud.

"That's the way it is," Grandmother answered. "That's the way it has always been in Bangladesh."

In Chayna's village, people were very poor. Some of them owned a little land on which they grew rice or sugar beets. But most people were laborers who had to work for others.

Chayna's family owned a small shop in the city. But the shop did not have much business, so one day Father came home and told the family he had sold it.

"But how will we earn a living?" asked Grandmother.

"I got a good price for the shop," Father answered.

"What will we do when we've used all that money?" asked Oloka.

This time Father shouted, "You women keep out of this!" Then he added softly, "Don't worry. Something will turn up."

Nearly one hundred million people live in Bangladesh. That's a lot of people for such a small country. Religion is very important to these people. Most of them believe in a god whose name is Allah, and in a great teacher whose name was Muhammed. Their holy book is called the Koran. It is filled with rules they must live by. These people are called Moslems.

But in the part of the country where Chayna lived, there were many people belonging to the Hindu religion. Hindus believe in many different kinds of gods. They have heard about these gods in the sagas and legends passed down by their parents. They believe the souls of people who die go on living in animals like cows or dogs or even rats, so they do not like to kill animals. Hindus have many strict rules to live by just like Moslems do. They are afraid the gods will punish them if they do not keep all the rules.

Chayna's family was Hindu. But one day a stranger came to visit their village. Father had heard about this man whom others called the evangelist. The evangelist claimed the Hindu gods were neither real nor alive. "They cannot help you at all," he told them, "no matter how much you sacrifice to them. They are only stones."

That frightened Grandmother. She whispered, "Be careful what you say. The gods may take revenge."

Others nodded, but the evangelist laughed out loud and said, "I am not afraid of those gods anymore. I have found one who is stronger, the living God, the only real God."

"What is his name?" asked Father.

"His name is Jesus Christ," the evangelist answered.

Everyone began to mumble, "Iesu Cris, Krishna Jesu." But Chayna heard the name of this new God very well, for she was sitting right in the front beside her father.

When the evangelist was ready to go, Chayna's father told him, "Your stories are interesting. Come back again."

But Chayna heard the Moslems in the village shout and throw stones after him, saying, "Stay away with your religion!"

Some of the village Hindus murmured, "The gods might punish us for listening to that man."

Chayna's father, however, and some of his neighbors stood around in clusters, talking about what they had heard. "Maybe we should do as the evangelist says and be baptized as Christians," they admitted.

Grandmother warned Chayna, "Watch out for the evil spirits that fly around between the cottages and hide in the trees."

Chayna trembled and grabbed onto a neighbor girl called Shefali. Then Father spoke up, "The evangelist says if we believe in Jesus and are baptized, we won't have to be afraid of evil spirits. He says Jesus is stronger."

"Do you believe in Jesus?" Shefali asked.

Grandmother hid her face in her dress while she waited for Father to answer.

"We want to learn more from the book he calls the Bible. We want the evangelist to come again. Yes, then we will decide if we want to be baptized."

The next month the evangelist came again. Many of the village people gathered to hear him read from the Bible. "Jesus loves us and gave His life for us," he exclaimed.

"Does He love girls too?" asked Chayna.

"Yes, He also loves you, little blossom," answered the evangelist with a hearty laugh. He looked right at Chayna. "When Jesus was here on earth he took special care of children and of all those whom others thought were not important, all those whom nobody wanted."

"What a strange god!" interrupted Grandmother.

"Jesus knows all about you, Grandmother," he continued. "And all about you, Chayna, and all about you," the evangelist said, pointing to Chayna's father. "If Jesus had not loved us exactly as we are, there would be no salvation. Do you think Allah wants you? Do you think the Hindu gods love you? No, of course not. But Jesus died for all of us in spite of our sins."

That Sunday morning Chayna, and her father, together with about half of the village people, came down to the well by the pond, dressed in their best clothes. The evangelist met them there. He had a pastor from another village with him. One by one the people waded into the water to be baptized. Although the water may not have been clean, Chayna felt she had been washed both inside and out.

Afterward, the people who had been baptized gathered near Chayna's hut for a meal together. Suddenly, there was shouting and scuffling in the village. A Muslim neighbor ran up to them shouting, "From now on, you don't get your water here at the village well. We won't share our water with Christians!" Then the man ran back the way he had come.

Chayna's father shouted after him, "We will get what we need from the river!"

But the women sighed and complained. They were the ones who would have to make the long walk to the river with heavy pots and jars. Chayna's mother was expecting another baby. It would be an especially long and hot walk for her.

Time passed. The river provided water for Chayna's family. But money for food was nearly gone. As the time grew closer for the new baby to be born, Chayna's mother grew weaker. One day she became very sick. She had been working too hard and eating too little. All day long she lay on her mat in the house, tossing and turning.

Chayna was nervous. She had a stomachache. She bit her nails. She was worried about Mother and she was worried the baby might be another girl.

Grandmother told Chayna, "If the baby is another girl, your father will have to look for another wife." Grandmother had not been baptized like the rest of the family, so she offered a cup of rice to the Hindu gods every day and prayed to them for a baby boy.

That afternoon Chayna left the hut and ran down to the pond to talk to the geese. She always did that when she was afraid. A flock of vultures sitting in a high tree caught her eye. "Go away!" she yelled as she picked up stones and threw them. But the vultures would not budge.

Chayna's father followed her. He squatted down beside her. "Are you afraid Mother is going to die?" he asked.

"Yes, and it's only because you want to have a boy!" Chayna cried. She hid her head between her knees. She expected her father to get mad and slap her.

But Father laid his arm around Chayna's shoulders. "Whether we get a boy or a girl is not important," he said quietly. "God will provide for us. He will give us just the right child."

Chayna looked up and nodded.

"I'm glad we have you, Chayna!" said her father.

Chayna smiled. "We can pray for Mother just like the evangelist taught us," she suggested.

But Oloka's voice broke their conversation. "Father, Chayna! Hurry! Hurry! The baby has come. It's a boy! A boy!"

Father and Chayna jumped into each other's arms.

Then Oloka continued, "But Mother is sick, very sick. She is. . . ."

Father and the girls took off running back to the hut, to Mother and the new baby boy. Grandmother met them at the door. "The baby is like a pretty blossom," she exclaimed.

"Yes," answered Father. "We'll call him **Kamalesh**, Lotus blossom for God!"

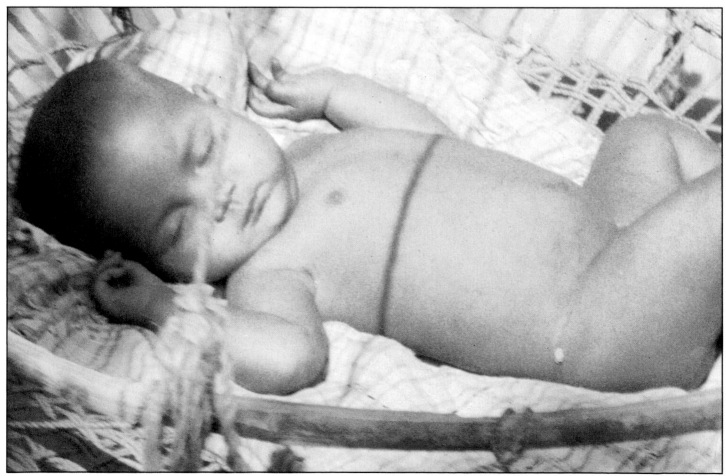

The following weeks Chayna was sent again and again to the river for water. Mother was still very sick. Father was having a hard time earning money for food. They had no money at all for medicine.

Chayna's father became desperate. The evangelist had once told him about a Christian school in the hills, a long journey by foot. Father decided to go there to ask for help. One of his neighbors went with him.

When, at last, they reached the school, Chayna's father nearly shouted, "We want to speak to **Sahib**, the master."

"Sahib? We don't call him 'Sahib,'" said the man they met outside. "We call him 'Brother.'"

"Okay, okay, just call him," said Chayna's father as he waved the man away.

Before long, a large white man came out to meet them. He had a long beard just like the Muslim priests, but he was carrying a little girl on his shoulders.

"**Nomoskar**!" he said with a big smile. That means "hello." The white man spoke their language.

Chayna's father told him, "We have not been allowed to use the village well ever since we were baptized as Christians. We need fresh water close by because my wife is very sick."

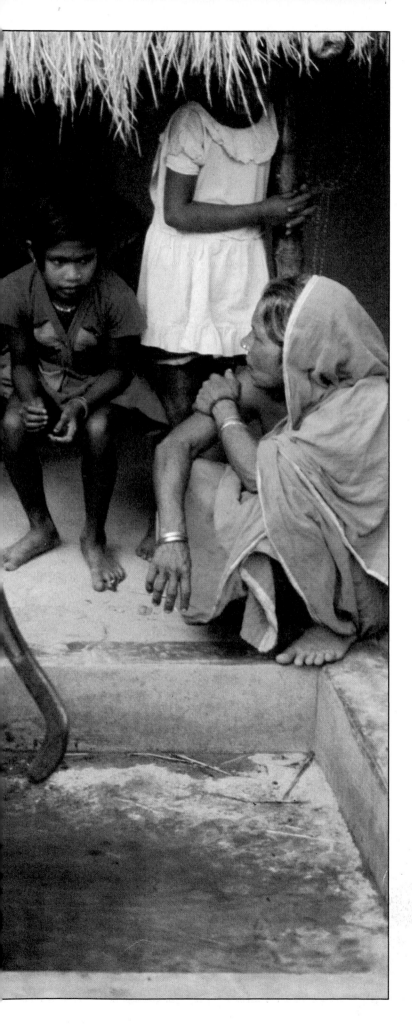

The missionary asked many questions. Chayna's father could not tell enough. He tried to tell the whole story at once.

Finally the missionary said, "We will help you. We will get you a hand pump for water, but you must find a piece of land in the center of town, and dig the bamboo pipe into the ground yourselves."

"Yes, yes," answered Chayna's father.

"And remember, anybody in the village must be allowed to use the pump, even the Moslems and Hindus."

"What?"

"Would Jesus ever have hindered His enemies from getting clean water?" asked the missionary.

Chayna's father had to admit the missionary was right. Tired, but happy, he started out once again down the long trail home. Only now, he and his neighbor were singing, laughing, and almost dancing as they went.

Within a few days the pump was delivered to the village. Chayna's father dug a hole in the earth and, with the neighbor's help, got the pump working. Now there was plenty of clean water close by.

But food was still hard to come by. Chayna's mother was not getting better, because she insisted the children eat what they needed first. She became thinner and weaker. One day she began to cough and shiver and sweat. She couldn't get up off her mat. Grandmother tried to get her to eat something, but it was too late. That night, Chayna's mother died.

Later that same month, the white missionary arrived in their village. "How is the water pump working?" he asked.

"My mother is dead," Chayna told him. "It is too late for your help!"

"But you can still help us," Grandmother interrupted. "We are all about to die of hunger."

The missionary was sad. He became very quiet. Then he took Chayna onto his lap. "Perhaps I can help the rest of you to help yourselves," he said. "Let me talk to the people in the village."

Once the people were gathered together, the evangelist said, "Bangladesh is a poor country, but I come from a country where there once was hunger and war. Then the people decided to help each other. They began to fight together against poverty and death."

The village people did not look at each other. They knew they had not been helping each other. "What do you mean?" they asked. "What can we do?"

"To begin with you can start a village school," answered the missionary. "Start by teaching each other what you already know!"

And that's what the people of Chayna's village did. They set up a blackboard right in the village square. Then they invited anyone who wanted to learn to read and write to come in the evenings, after their work was done. Chayna's father was the only one who could already read a little, so he was appointed teacher. The missionary gave him books to read and to write in.

Some of the older men taught ironsmith and carpentry classes for the boys. The girls were taught to weave baskets that could be sold in the city.

The missionary loaned the village school some money sent by the church in his homeland to produce a kind of peanut snack called **Chanachur.** People in Bangladesh love to eat Chanachur, so it is easy to sell. Chayna and her sisters learned to make it out of bean meal, roasted peanuts and strong spices. Their neighbor Shefali helped. They pressed the dough through a sieve into a pan of boiling oil to make crispy sticks. Then they mixed these sticks with roasted peanuts and packed it into small bags.

But Shefali found it difficult to concentrate on making Chanachur. Shefali was dreaming about her wedding. In a few days she would become married to a man she had never seen. Her parents had arranged the marriage with his parents and planned a big wedding feast. Shefali was both excited and nervous. There were going to be many people, all dressed up, all happy for her.

Chayna couldn't help feeling envious. She had been to a wedding once before. There had been more food than anyone could possibly eat: goat meat, fish, rice, yogurt and candy. The bride had worn a beautiful new dress that the bridegroom had given her. Her face had been painted as if with tiny red and white flower petals. She had looked radiant. Chayna looked forward to the time when she would marry and have children. "And I'll be sure to have lots of baby boys," she thought to herself.

Chayna loved going to the evening classes in her village, even though they were supposed to be for grownups. She learned to read and write quickly. One day her father took her to the mission boarding school in the hills. He wanted her to learn more than she could learn in the village school. He knew Chayna was an eager student with a sharp mind.

The teachers at the school allowed Chayna to start second grade when they heard she could already read and write. At first, Chayna was sorry to leave her grandmother, her sisters, and her little brother at home. But she made friends at the school just as quickly as she learned. And she played just as eagerly as she studied. In Bangladesh, not many people can afford to buy toys, so children make their own toys out of wood or clay or odds and ends they find. They play jumping and dancing games. Sometimes they just pretend they are great big animals.

Each morning, the school children lined up in rows outside the classroom. They sang their national song with all their hearts as the flag of Bangladesh was raised. Chayna's eyes always filled with tears when she sang, "My golden Bangladesh, I love you. . ."

Chayna thrived at school. She especially enjoyed sitting on real wooden benches, instead of on the ground like they did at home. Her teachers were kind and patient. And she was given a school uniform and school books! She did not know which she liked best, reading, writing, arithmetic, social studies, music, or geography. She finally decided she liked studying the Bible best of all.

At school Chayna was given three meals a day, and meat for supper at least once a week. Chayna's cheeks became rosy, and a new light sparkled in her eyes. She remembered the times as a small child when she had often gone hungry. She knew there were thousands of villages in Bangladesh where children still went hungry, or had only a little rice to eat. Chayna knew many children would die because they could not get medicine or help in time.

Chayna often thought about the first time the evangelist had come to their village. She would never forget the first time she had felt the love of Jesus Christ, the one true God.

One day Chayna's father visited the school. "Are you happy, Chayna?" he asked. "Are you studying hard?"

"Of course, Father!" Chayna beamed. "I want to become a nurse. I want to help others live better, learn about Jesus, and feel important."

Chayna's father was very proud. He looked back at the teacher and said, "That's my Chayna!"